SNOWBOY and the LAST TREE STANDING

For Santino Ray Oram and his dad — H. O.

For my afi Guðmundur, who I planted trees with — B. S.

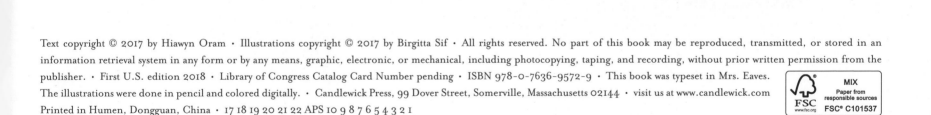

Text copyright © 2017 by Hiawyn Oram · Illustrations copyright © 2017 by Birgitta Sif · All rights reserved. No part of this book may be reproduced, transmitted, or stored in an information retrieval system in any form or by any means, graphic, electronic, or mechanical, including photocopying, taping, and recording, without prior written permission from the publisher. · First U.S. edition 2018 · Library of Congress Catalog Card Number pending · ISBN 978-0-7636-9572-9 · This book was typeset in Mrs. Eaves. The illustrations were done in pencil and colored digitally. · Candlewick Press, 99 Dover Street, Somerville, Massachusetts 02144 · visit us at www.candlewick.com Printed in Humen, Dongguan, China · 17 18 19 20 21 22 APS 10 9 8 7 6 5 4 3 2 1

FSC MIX Paper from responsible sources FSC® C101537

SNOWBOY and the LAST TREE STANDING

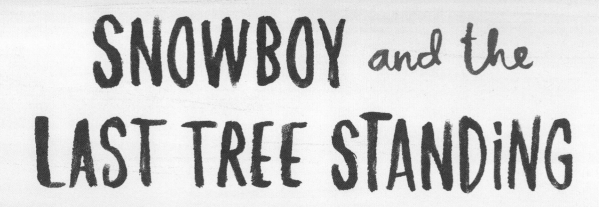

Hiawyn Oram

illustrated by Birgitta Sif

CANDLEWICK PRESS

Snowboy and his Ice Troopers

were saving the Polar Bear King from the
Evil One-Eyed Emperor when Greenbackboy came up.

"I know a better game than this," he said.
"It's called KA-CHING, and it starts in the forests."

"OK," said Snowboy. "I'll bring my Cloak of Many Uses."

The forests were dark.
Greenbackboy's eyes lit
them like moonlight.

"OK," said Greenbackboy.
"This is the game. We cut down all the trees.
Here's your ax."

When nearly all the trees were gone,
Snowboy thought, *We can't breathe without trees.*
And he left one standing, hidden by
his Cloak of Many Uses.

"OK," said Greenbackboy.

"All the trees have gone to be made into things.

In return for them we got this.

Look!

Piles and piles of KA-CHING.

With it we can get anything we want.

But we want more. So on to the oceans."

The oceans were deep and ever moving.
Greenbackboy's eyes lit them like lighthouses.
"Now," he said, "we catch all the fish. Here's your net."

When nearly all the fish were caught,

Snowboy thought,

What's a sea without fish?

A dead sea, that's what.

And he let two slip free when

Greenbackboy wasn't watching.

"OK," said Greenbackboy.
"The fish have gone to be canned.
In return we got more KA-CHING than
anyone could ever dream of. With it we can—"
But in that moment a terrible storm
blew up, drowning his words.

As there were no trees to snag its wings, it swept all before it,
tossing the mountains of canned fish into the empty oceans,
where they sank and rusted and were lost.

"Back to Level Nowhere," said Snowboy. "Now what?"

"No worries," said Greenbackboy. "We're still the KA-CHING kings. I kept it all safe in my strongbox."

"Thanks," said Snowboy. "But it's no good to us now. We can't breathe KA-CHING. We can't eat KA-CHING. And I've got to get going."

He gathered his Ice Troopers and the Polar Bear King,
and together they trudged across the wrecked land
until they reached the last tree standing,
saved from the storm by the Cloak of Many Uses.

Gently and lovingly, they nursed
it out of its loneliness and
charmed a swarm of bees
to build a hive
in its branches.

They made a boat
and went to sea and saw
that the last two fish
had had lots of little fish
who were growing up
to have little fish
of their own.

And when they got back to their tree,
they found one of its seeds had taken root.
"Hurrah!" said Snowboy. "Two will become
many, many millions. Good work, Team Us!

But wait. . . .

Who's this limping along?"

It was Greenbackboy, looking pale and as thin as a stick.
"You were right, Snowboy," he said, sniffling. "You can't eat KA-CHING, and I'm starving."

"Then you're in luck," said Snowboy, showing him the beehive.
"There's honey. But ask nicely and leave some for tomorrow, or you will be hungry again."

And with that, Snowboy spread his cloak.
As it was a Cloak of Many Uses it flew them home,
where Snowboy fell happily asleep, knowing he and his team
had saved the world from the fantasy of KA-CHING . . .

for now at least.